FUN WITH THE PROFESSORS

A Pleasure Collection Story

Jash Kol-Ze

Cover design by: Jash Kol-Ze

Printed in the United States of America

Dedicated to Cardinal,
The most wonderful succulent.

CONTENTS

PREFACE

This story is supposed to be fun with a barely there plot.

There is a chance that this story may be triggering to some. Stacey is much younger than the two professors referenced in the book's title. They also start having sex with her without warning.

FUN WITH THE PROFESSORS

I looked at myself in the mirror and let out a groan. As a joke the previous day I had bought a sexy schoolgirl outfit. Since I had bought it a few sizes too big, it didn't really look sexy. The joke was supposed to be that I would look totally unappealing to the two professors I had crushes on. But since the outfit had shrunk in the washer, I now looked too appealing.

My tits had been bigger than average when I was sixteen and were still some of the biggest now that I was nineteen. They were currently pressing hard against my shirt leaving my black laced bra highly exposed. The skirt barely covered my cunt. Hopefully I didn't move the wrong way or else everyone would be able to see I wasn't currently wearing any panties.

"Shit!" I screamed as I looked at the time.

I quickly put on sneakers, in the hopes that they would somehow diminish my sex appeal, and raced out of my dorm room. Then I raced back in when I realized I had forgotten my backpack.

* * *

I walked through the halls of the campus. It was my third semester here so there was no real need for me to focus. Honestly it was better not to focus as people around me tended to gawk at my outfit. It didn't help that my bra barely stopped my tits from going up and down as I walked.

What if Professor Hendricks with his light stubble found me like this? He was the only reason algebra was worth failing a third time. What if Professor Kane with his tanned body and clean shaven face saw me? Even though I was an adult, they were still my teachers.

"Fuck this shit." I said and grasped at the sides of a drinking fountain after putting my backpack down. "Stacey Anderson, you're better than this. You're going to go to all your classes today and then forget this day ever happened."

As I began to drink from the drinking fountain, I felt a strong hand start to go up my skirt and then realized someone had walked up behind me. Before I could do anything, he began to rub my clit with his finger. I moaned loudly and distantly felt my body lean forward.

"Miss Anderson," Professor Hendricks' throaty voice said as he continued to bring me closer to the edge. "You shouldn't be wearing that."

"Yes." I managed to say between my moans.

"What should I do about that?"

Suddenly I was about to cum and then he brought me back down. I cried out. For an eternity I thought he would leave me in this state of eternal torment. Then, blessedly, he brought me tumbling over the edge with pleasure I never thought possible. I came multiple times and cried out louder.

When I came down I realized my shirt was wet and the hunk

Hendricks had fucked me with his finger. I had been fucked before but never so well with one finger. With a blush on my face I picked myself up and turned around to the sight of Hendricks sucking off my juices from his finger.

And a large group of students gathered in the hallway.

"I'm sorry." I said weakly and put my arms over my chest.

"Sorry?" Hendricks replied with a chuckle.

"Yeah..."

"So you don't want to fuck me?"

"No..."

Of course I wanted to! If he could do so much with a finger..fuck! But I couldn't say that in front of the others. Not even though he had fingered me to multiple orgasms in front of witnesses.

With a sly grin on his lips he walked to one of the girls standing near the front of the crowd. Beth's bright blue eyes looked at Hendricks with desire. He must have fucked her before. I thought it was only a joke that he would fuck some of the students. At least those nineteen and above. Usually above. Beth was twenty-one and wearing clothes that did her curves no favors. At least in my opinion.

In a series of quick motions Hendricks ripped her shirt off, started squeezing her tits, and slammed her against a wall. Even though Beth had to have been lost in ecstasy, I knew I was, she managed to pull her pants down. She then pulled his pants and underwear down.

A growl was my only warning before he shoved his cock deep inside her. I watched as he fucked her hard. In under a minute both Beth and myself had cum multiple times. Hendricks slowed down his thrusts when he turned to look at me.

Now was my chance to do the right thing. Now was my chance to walk away and go back to my dorm. But I was so wet and my cunt needed his cock. That thing that was still leaving Beth in a state of bliss.

Fuck it!

I nervously took off my shirt as Hendricks' eyes bore into my tits. I slowly took off my shoes, socks, and skirt as he licked his lips at the wetness between my legs. I took off my bra and let it fall to the floor as the math professor lost all of his humanity.

Hendricks let Beth fall to the floor, her smile was the only indication she was fine, and raced towards me. His lips sucked my tits as he fingered me. He brought me to the edge but kept holding me back. I cried out but to no avail.

"What are you doing?" Professor Kane yelled but Hendricks didn't seem to notice. "Fuck her already!"

What?

With a growl Hendricks guided us both to the floor and positioned me above him. I blushed at Kane right as he started undressing himself. I couldn't tell which professor had the bigger cock. Well, there was no going back now. Even if I could back out...I didn't want to.

Gritting my teeth, I shoved the massive cock inside of me. The moment it was in me I started fucking him as the ecstasy was overwhelming. Hendricks' hands held me steady as my movements were erratic. Oh god! This was so good! Oh my fuck, he's helping me!

My back arched as I came and a loud cry of pleasure exited my lips. My back stayed arched as another wave of pleasure followed. I managed to look down and saw Hendricks playing with my clit. That sent me spiraling into even more waves of orgasms that just wouldn't stop. And I didn't want them to!

I closed my eyes and opened them when I felt warm cum on my tits and back. A loud moan left my lips as I realized what was happening. Kane's tan and fit form was walking around to my back. The sight of me riding his colleague was enough to make him cum.

Suddenly I wasn't shy anymore. I loved that people were being turned on by me. I loved that I was actually getting fucked by the two hottest professors on campus!

Hendricks helped steady me when Kane entered me from behind. The pleasure was so intense that it was difficult not to fall down. After a few minutes we found a rhythm. Both men's hands and lips touched every inch of my skin that they could. Hendricks preferred my tits and Kane favored my neck.

It seemed like the pleasure would never end until it did. After we experienced one final orgasm, we collapsed on each other.

"You wear that outfit again and we'll give you a proper detention." Hendricks said with a grin.

"Both of us will." Kane added.

"What about extra credit?" I teased.

"Don't push it." Kane laughed.

AFTERWORD

I hope you had as much fun reading this story as I had writing it.

THE PLEASURE COLLECTION

Have you just read a book that tore at your heartstrings? Are you having a hard day?

The Pleasure Collection is here to provide you with stories that seek only to...er...bring a smile to your face.

Fun With The Professors

Stacey Anderson decided to buy an oversized outfit as a joke. But when the washer shrank it things seem headed in a bad direction.

Things get even worse when something happens at a drinking fountain.

But maybe all hope isn't lost and Stacey will end the day with good memories.

Fun with the Professors is an erotic short story that's part of the Pleasure Collection.

BOOKS IN THIS SERIES

Kafka's Men

Corvid "Kafka" Ravenhart has no past or future. All she has is the present trying to escape the Cassowary Institute.

What is the Cassowary Institute? How did Kafka become involved with them? All she knows is that they gave her superhuman abilities and trained her to fight for them. She doesn't know how she first became involved with them.

Even while thinking she has no hope of finally living her own life, she still manages to find love. But will love be enough?

Kafka's Men is a slow burning Reverse Harem series.

Forget Thyself

It all begins with a scream...

Corvid "Kafka" Ravenhart gives herself amnesia for a chance at survival. While that might increase her chances for survival in the future, in the present it leaves her vulnerable to an enemy she has no name for.

The only kind face she meets is Blaine Rue. But it's just as likely the dashing man will be her downfall as much as her salvation.

Forget Thyself is the first book in the slow burning Reverse Harem series Kafka's Men.

That Which Remains

What is love...

Corvid "Kafka" Ravenhart has a lot to think about. She has amnesia and yet the Cassowary Institute expects her to perform like she doesn't. A mistake on the wrong test could spell the end of her short life.

Yet even though she should be fully focused on Institute business, Kafka can't help but wonder how her relationship with Blaine Rue began. Why did the other woman decide to start sleeping with him? Did she ever truly love him?

Does it even matter?

That Which Remains is the second book in the slow burning Reverse Harem series Kafka's Men.

And The Band Played On

A secret will be discovered...

Corvid "Kafka" Ravenhart considers herself separate from the other woman. She thinks of the other woman as more of a mother than who she was before. Most days Kafka doesn't even mind how much of the other woman's memories she doesn't have.

But when Kafka gets the feeling that she's partially in morph, she wishes that she had more of the other woman's memories.

And The Band Played On is the third book in the slow burning Reverse Harem series Kafka's Men.

A Date With The Devil

One special night...

Corvid "Kafka" Ravenhart has grown used to her relationship with Blaine Rue. She understands that their relationship can never be normal as he is the one keeping her caged.

So she is surprised when Blaine decides to have a date night with her.

For one magical night Kafka gets to experience a part of humanity she never thought she'd be able to.

A Date with the Devil is the fourth book in the slow burning Reverse Harem series Kafka's Men.

BOOKS IN THIS SERIES

A Reason to Live For

By accident Artra survived the great disaster that killed everyone else of her kind. She hid in shame only after the Great Enemy was destroyed. Now, eons later, the Great Enemy has once again showed its ugly face and Artra hides among humans as she fights. Whether this is to fool her foe or because she is still ashamed, she does not know.

Artra's world is shattered when she meets Frank Axis.

A Reason to Live For is a steamy Reverse Harem series.

Everything Changes

Artra is the last of an ancient race of shapeshifters who has finally decided to come out of hiding once the Great Enemy, called the First by humans, finds a way to resurrect itself.

To fight her ancient foe, she joins the prestigious ship the Persephone as its new pilot. She also pretends to be human and takes on the alias Anita Armstrong.

Artra finds a certain kind of peace mixed with loneliness as she continues the good fight. But when a standard salvage mission goes awry, she finds that for love she will have to change.

Everything Changes is the first book in the Reverse Harem series A Reason to Live For.

Cost Of Honesty

Artra is happier than she has been in eons. Even though the war with the Great Enemy rages on, she has found love in the arms of the legendary hero Frank Axis.

Yet there is something holding her back from true happiness: honesty.

If she does tell Frank the truth, Artra runs the risk of destroying the peace she has managed to find for herself. But if she continues to lie can she truly ever love Frank?

Cost of Honesty is the second book in the Reverse Harem series A Reason to Live For.

ABOUT THE AUTHOR

Jash Kol-Ze

Jash Kol-Ze lives in Florida with her husband and three birds. She always had a love of writing which she pursued by going to Saint Leo University. She graduated with a Bachelor of Arts in English with a Specialization in Creative Writing.

Jash spends the majority of her days helping around the house and working on her blog.

You can find her blog at jashykins.blogspot.com

www.ingramcontent.com/pod-product-compliance
Lightning Source LLC
LaVergne TN
LVHW020546160826
845677LV00015B/4236

* 9 7 9 8 8 4 3 9 7 1 9 0 8 *